猴
Monkey

雞
Rooster

豬
Pig

羊
Sheep

For nearly 5,000 years, the Chinese culture has organized time in cycles of twelve years. This Eastern calendar is based upon the movement of the moon (as compared to the Western which follows the sun), and is symbolized by the zodiac circle. An animal that has unique qualities represents each year. Therefore, if you are born in a particular year, then you share the personality of that animal. Now people worldwide celebrate this two-week long festival in the early spring and enjoy the start of another Chinese New Year.

馬
Horse

鼠
Rat

蛇
Snake

牛
Ox

龍
Dragon

兔
Rabbit

虎
Tiger

To Amy, Lucas, Eli, and all the friends we've met along the journey.
We appreciate all your support!
—O.C.

Dedicated to Juan Agustin & Ian Mateo.
—J.C.

To Isla, our little snake.
—E.L.J.

immedium

Immedium, Inc.
P.O. Box 31846
San Francisco, CA 94131
www.immedium.com

www.liberumdonum.com

Text Copyright © 2017 Oliver Chin
Illustrations Copyright © 2017 Juan Calle (Liberum Donum studios)

First hardcover edition published 2017. Second printing February 2017.
Edited by Don Menn
Book design by Erica Loh Jones
Chinese translation by Hsiaoying Chen

Printed in Malaysia
10 9 8 7 6 5 4 3 2

Library of Congress Cataloging-in-Publication Data

Names: Chin, Oliver Clyde, 1969-, author. | Calle, Juan, 1977-, illustrator.
Title: The year of the rooster : tales from the Chinese zodiac / by Oliver Chin ; illustrated by Juan Calle.
Description: San Francisco : Immedium, Inc., 2017. | Summary: "The young rooster Ray befriends the girl Ying, as well as other
    animals of the Chinese lunar calendar, and demonstrates the qualities of a confident adventurer. Lists the birth years and
    characteristics of individuals born in the Chinese Year of the Rooster"-- Provided by publisher.
Identifiers: LCCN 2016011649 (print) | LCCN 2016032293 (ebook) | ISBN 9781597021258 (hardback) | ISBN 1597021253
    (hardcover) | ISBN 9781597021272 | ISBN 159702127X
Subjects: | CYAC: Roosters--Fiction. | Self-confidence--Fiction. | Animals--Fiction. | Astrology, Chinese--Fiction. | BISAC: JUVENILE
    FICTION / People & Places / United States / Asian American. | JUVENILE FICTION / Animals / Birds. | JUVENILE FICTION /
    Holidays & Celebrations / Other, Non-Religious.
Classification: LCC PZ7.C44235 Yes 2017 (print) | LCC PZ7.C44235 (ebook) | DDC [E]--dc23 LC record available at
    https://lccn.loc.gov/2016011649

ISBN 978-1-59702-125-8

The Year of the Rooster
Tales from the Chinese Zodiac
十二生肖故事系列 鸡年的故事

文：陈曜豪 Written by Oliver Chin

图：胡安·卡雷 Illustrated by Juan Calle

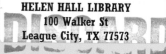
immedium
www.immedium.com
San Francisco, CA

Another year began, and a family of chickens was very excited. Three weeks ago, the hen had laid an egg and kept it warm in her nest. As her caring husband hovered about, she felt its shell start to crack.

又是一年的开始，鸡的一家充满着欢欣的气象。在三个星期以前，母鸡妈妈下了一个蛋，从那个时候起，她就小心翼翼地把它放在鸡窝里保持温暖。公鸡爸爸寸步不离地围在窝边。这时，鸡妈妈觉得蛋壳像是要破了。

Soon their baby was hopping around the chicken coop. **"Peep peep,"** he chirped.

Happily he skipped in the sun
and made their lives brighter.
"Let's name him Ray,"
proposed Papa, and Mama agreed.

过了不久，就见到他们的小鸡宝宝在鸡栏边跳来跳去。"叽叽，"小鸡叫着。

小鸡高兴地在太阳底下蹦蹦跳跳，他的出生为他的父母带来了光亮。"我们就叫他小磊吧！"鸡爸爸提议，鸡妈妈也同意了。

Their neighbor Ying came to clean their coop. She brought fresh feed, water, and straw. Ruffling Ray's downy coat, Ying laughed, "You're a cutie!" They played "chicken" and he liked her right away.

他们的邻居小英过来帮忙打扫鸡舍。她还带来了新鲜的饲料、水和稻草。小英拨弄着小磊身上的羽毛，笑着说："你真可爱啊！"他们一起玩小鸡游戏，而小磊马上就喜欢上了小英。

Each day Mama rustled the growing chick out of bed for breakfast.
Yet Papa always had finished his work and come home.
Ray wondered, **"Where does he go every morning?"**

"You'll see," replied Mama.

每天早上，鸡妈妈都会把小鸡从被窝里叫起，让他起床吃早餐。但是，鸡爸爸总是得先做完他的工作才回家。小磊觉得奇怪，心想，"爸爸每天早上都到什么地方去了？"

"有一天你会知道的，"鸡妈妈回答。

Then before one dawn, Ray was shaken from his dreams. His father whispered, "Son, come with me."

"It is still dark outside," yawned Ray. But Papa led him across the courtyard and up to the bell tower.

于是，在某一天的黎明之前，小磊从睡梦中被人摇醒。他的爸爸轻声道："儿子，跟我来。"

"外面还黑着呢，"小磊打着呵欠说。但爸爸还是带着他穿过了庭院，然后跃上钟楼。

Patiently they waited until the sun peeked over the horizon.
Then the rooster loudly crowed, "Cock-a-doodle-doo!"

Lights dotted the homes below. The dog barked, "Bow wow."
The community rose to greet the day.

他们耐心地等候着，一直等到太阳从水平线升起。这时公鸡大声地鸣叫："喔喔喔！"
阳光照亮地面上的房舍。狗叫着："汪汪。"整个城镇都起床迎接新的一天的来临。

"Your job is to wake the town up!" marveled Ray.

Papa bragged, "Yes, and one day you'll do it too." Just then a second flash startled them. A commotion rippled across town, so Papa and Ray hurried to the square.

"原来你的工作是把镇上的人们和动物们叫醒阿！"小磊惊奇地说。
鸡爸爸夸耀："是的！而且阿，将来这也会是你的工作。"

这个时候，天边突然出现了一道闪光，他们都吓了一跳。镇上传来一阵喧闹，
于是鸡爸爸和小磊就急急忙忙忙地赶到了市中心广场。

A crowd swirled around the pig, who yelled, "I saw the phoenix!" They scoffed since no one had ever seen the legendary animal. "I have proof!" she cried and raised a red feather that silenced the throng.

在广场上，群众围绕着小猪。小猪说："我看到了一只凤凰！"没有人见过凤凰这种传奇动物，大家都不相信小猪说的话，嘲笑着她。"我有证据！"小猪大声说，然后一面举起一根红色的羽毛。这时大家都安静了下来，没有人再说话。

The quill was similar to Ray's but shone like a ruby. Was it from someone like him? Amazed, he sped home and announced, **"I want to see the phoenix!"**

Knocked off her perch, Mama replied, "Don't pull my leg."

那根羽毛看起来和小磊身上的羽毛相似，但是它的光泽却像红宝石那样的闪亮。这羽毛是从像他一样的动物身上来的吗？他觉得惊奇。他用飞快的速度跑回家，跟家人宣布："我要去找凤凰！"

鸡妈妈撞倒了她的栖木，回答："不要开我玩笑了！"

Papa cautioned, "We may not be birds of the same feather."

But Ying was curious and said, "I'll go with him."

鸡爸爸警告着小鸡："我们和凤凰是不一样的鸟类。"

但是小英却感到好奇，她说："我要跟小磊一块儿去。"

So the youngsters set off to find the phoenix.
A rat told them to visit the farmers market to learn the latest news.

于是，小磊就和小英一起离开家去找寻凤凰。一只老鼠告诉他们可以去农夫市场打听最新的消息。

There they came upon a hot and weary ox.
Ray kindly brought it a drink.

The ox wheezed, "Thanks! I rushed back
after I discovered this in the field..."
She revealed a white feather that
gleamed like ivory.

在那儿，他们遇到了一头又热又累的牛。小磊好心地拿了些水给她。
牛喘着气说："谢谢！我发现了这个东西以后，急忙从田里赶回来……"她拿出
了一根像象牙般白得发亮的羽毛。

"The phoenix wears five colors," stated the ox. "White symbolizes the tiger."
She gazed toward the jungle beyond. Now Ying hesitated to leave the city.
But the cocky chicken crossed the road to get to the other side.

"凤凰的羽毛有五种颜色，"
牛说。"白色是老虎的颜色阿。"小英望
向丛林的深处。现在小英开始犹豫了，她想她
到底要不要离开这个城镇继续向前。但这只充满
自信的小鸡已经走过了马路，到了路的另一头。

"Could the mythical beast resemble a tiger?" whispered Ying. Entering the thick brush, the pair lost the trail. Suddenly they heard a fearsome roar!

Quivering in fear, Ray meekly cooed, **"Cock-a-doo!"**

"这个神秘的怪兽会不会是老虎呢?"小英轻声说。
当他们进入灌木丛的时候,他们迷路了。
突然间,他们听到了一声可怕的吼叫声。
小磊吓得发抖,他发出微弱的叫声:"喔喔喔!"

From the shadows, a mighty cat emerged. Swallowing his pride,
Ray asked, **"Are you the phoenix?"**

The tiger smiled. "No, but it passed through here. Follow me."
He guided them to the jungle's edge and bade farewell.

一只大猫从树荫里走出来。小磊提起勇气问：
"你就是那只凤凰吗？"
老虎笑着说："我不是，但是凤凰曾经从这里经过。跟我
走吧。"他带领着他们走到了丛林的尽头，然后就离开了。

The kids scanned the meadow ahead.
The tall grass swayed. Ying shouted,
"Something is coming!"

"What is it?" squawked Ray.
Out bounded a rabbit. She clutched
a green feather that sparkled
like an emerald.

孩子们看着前面的牧草地。长长的牧草摆动了起来。
小英大喊："有东西要过来了！"

"是什么东西阿？"小磊粗声地问。一只兔子从草丛里跳
了出来。她拿着一根颜色像绿宝石一般闪亮的绿羽毛。

The bunny explained, "The phoenix looks like different animals. Its tail flaps like a fish." The rabbit showed them the brook where she found the feather. From there, Ray and Ying tracked the stream to a lake.

兔子解释:"凤凰和其他的动物长得不一样。她能拍动她的尾巴,就像鱼拍动鱼尾那样。"兔子带着他们来到她找到羽毛的小河。小磊和小英沿着小河走,走到了一片湖泊。

From the shore, they spied a colorful creature swimming in the distance. "Is it the fabled phoenix?" guessed Ying. They waved and a grand serpent approached them.

Ray called out, **"Are these your feathers?"**

他们在湖岸边发现一只色彩缤纷的动物在远处的水里游来游去。"这就是那传说中的凤凰吗？"小英猜想。他们向他挥了挥手，而这条巨大的蛇就朝他们的方向靠近。

小磊大声喊："这是你的羽毛吗？"

"No, they are from my old friend," answered the dragon. Inspecting the plumes, he noted, "The phoenix wanders at night. I'll bring you to one of her favorite places." He helpfully ferried them to the far shore.

"不是！那是我一个老朋友的羽毛。"龙回答。仔细看看这些羽毛以后，他解释："凤凰都在晚上的时候行动。我带你们去一个她平时爱去的地方。"他帮助他们游过湖泊，载着他们来到远端的湖岸。

The dragon said the phoenix symbolized heavenly bodies. Gazing at the stars,
they noticed a shadow approach. Ray squeaked, **"Cock-a-doodle!"**
It was a horse, who held a black feather that twinkled like an opal.

龙告诉他们，凤凰象征着天上运行的星球。他们望着天上的星星，发现有个阴影朝
他们接近。小磊叫出声音："喔喔喔！"原来是一匹马，他拿着一根黑色的羽毛。那
黑色的羽毛，像蛋白石一样一闪一闪的。

The horse whispered, "The phoenix's neck represents the moon and curves like a snake's." Indeed, the snake lived in the next valley. Luckily the horse was headed that direction and offered to carry them.

马轻声地说："凤凰的脖子象征着月亮，而那脖子的样子也跟蛇的脖子一样，弯弯的。"的确，蛇就住在隔壁的山谷。很辛运地，马正好要往那个方向去，他能顺便载他们一程。

In the morning, they spotted the snake on the path.
Checking the feathers, she hissed, "S-s-sorry, they aren't mine."

Ying asked, "What should we do now?"

"Maybe we should go back home," sighed Ray.

早晨的时候，他们在小径上发现了蛇。看了看羽毛之后，
蛇回答："真抱歉，这些不是我的羽毛。"

小英问："我们现在要怎么办呢？"
"或许我们该回家了，"小磊叹了口气说。

But the snake encouraged them, "Seeing the phoenix is good luck. If you find her, your quest will be well worth it." Heartened, the travelers pressed onward until they came upon a flock of grazing sheep.

然而，蛇却为他们加油打气，他说："见到凤凰会给你带来好运。如果你们真的能找到她，一切的辛苦就都值得了。"他们两个鼓起勇气继续向前，他们到了一片牧草地，并在那里碰到一大群羊。

A glint caught Ray's eye. Stuck in the carpet of wool was a yellow feather. It glowed like gold. Ray exclaimed, **"Where did you get this?"**

"I think you know," the sheep responded and gave it to him.

小磊的目光被一抹光亮吸引。一根黄色的羽毛卡在软绵绵的羊毛上。那金亮的羽毛明晃晃的，就像黄金一样。小磊惊呼："你在哪里找到这个的？""我想你知道的，"羊回答了之后就把羽毛交给小磊。

"The phoenix embodies five great virtues,"
she added. "One is knowledge,
which you are gaining."

She tapped Ray's big bird brain.
The sheep continued,
"The monkey is clever too,
so get his advice."

"凤凰象征五种良好的美德，"她又说。
"其中一种是知识，就是你现在正在学习
的。"她拍拍小磊聪明的脑袋。

羊又继续说："猴子也很聪明的，别忘了
去问问他能给你什么建议。"

Ying glimpsed a monkey swinging in the forest. Drawing near Ray hollered, **"Have you seen the phoenix?"**

The monkey chuckled and pointed high above. "Go climb this mountain. What you seek may lie up there."

小英瞥见森林里有一只猴子在树上荡来荡去。小磊靠近猴子并大声问:"你见过凤凰吗?"

猴子咯咯地笑着,他指向高处。"到这座山上去。你找寻的东西或许就在上头呢。"

The friends took a deep breath and tackled the towering hike. Many obstacles lay before them, but they did not give up. Often they paused to rest and enjoy the views. Then they trekked into the night.

这对朋友深深地吸了一口气后，就爬上那高耸的山。他们遭遇到了很多的困难和阻碍，但是都没有放弃。他们经常停下来休息，欣赏沿路的美景。他们慢慢地走，天色也渐渐地暗了。

Cresting the
last ridge, the girl
and the little rooster
could feel a warm light
rising from the sky.

Ray felt a strange sensation.
A sizzle swelled within his
chest. Ray boldly crowed,
"Cock-a-doodle-doo!"

到达山顶的时候，女孩和小公鸡发现
一道温暖的光芒从天空射出。小磊察觉
自己有种奇妙的感受。嘶嘶的声音在他
的胸膛鼓起。小磊放声大叫："喔喔喔！"

Ying and Ray faced the phoenix! Its eyes blazed like the sun. Its coat shimmered like a rainbow of gems. She praised both her cousin and his pal, "You've displayed a fiery spirit and have a bright future ahead."

小英和小磊见到了凤凰！她的眼睛像太阳一样灿烂。她身上的羽毛就像七彩宝石一样。她夸赞了她的远亲表弟小磊和他的朋友，说："你们对你们相信的事物充满着热情，还有着不怕困难的勇气，我相信你们的未来会是美好的。"

Overjoyed that his long journey was almost over, Ray had another idea! Politely he requested, **"Could you tell that to our parents?"**

"Sure thing!" twittered the phoenix and flew the delighted companions back to town.

小磊沉浸在他即将结束旅行的喜悦，这时，他有了另外一个主意！他有礼貌地请求凤凰："你能把你告诉我的这些说给我的家人听吗？"

"当然没问题！"凤凰轻笑着说，然后她就载着两位伙伴回到镇上。

When they arrived, everyone was amazed. Mama and Papa were pleased that their chick had come home to roost. Ray had made a once-in-a-lifetime trip. He'd cherish all the characters he met along the way.

他们回到镇上的时候，大家都感到惊讶。鸡爸爸和鸡妈妈很高兴他们的孩子终于回家休息了。小磊经历了一场难得的旅程。他会珍惜所有他在路上遇到的这些人物。

Returning to his daily routine, Ray dutifully respected the pecking order
and remembered to practice his chicken scratch.
But he still loved to have fun with Ying and stir things up.

回到他原本的生活以后，小磊乖乖地遵守鸡家族长幼有序的家规，
他也不忘练习写他那大家都看不懂的鸡画符。但他还是喜欢和
小英一起开心地玩，一起捣蛋闹事。

Searching for the phoenix always inspired Ray to fly high and dig deep.

And everyone truly agreed that it was a Happy Year of the Rooster.

通过这个找寻凤凰的经历，小磊得到了很大的启发，他相信要肯定自己，做事情也要尽力而为。

而大家都同意，今年是快乐的鸡年。

雞

Rooster 生肖鸡

1921, 1933, 1945, 1957, 1969, 1981, 1993, 2005, 2017, 2029

People born in the Year of the Rooster are confident, practical, and talented. They are diligent, observant, and vocal. But they can be dramatic or prideful, and like to show off. Though their egos can swell, roosters follow their instincts and are partners you can count on.

在鸡年出生的人是充满自信、实际而且有才华的。他们有勤奋努力、观察敏锐且直言不讳的个性。但有些时候,他们的情绪反应大,有时过度自傲且喜于表现自己。虽然鸡的自我意识很强,他们也总是跟着自己的直觉走,但他们是值得信赖的伙伴。